Who Killed the Mince Spy?

A Food Related Crime Investigation

Matthew Redford

Published by Clink Street Publishing 2016

Copyright © 2016

First edition.

ISBN: 978-1-911525-15-8
Ebook: 978-1-911525-16-5

For my friends Sally and Ian…

…they know me well, which is why I keep them close…

Contents

1

The no fan of fan ovens fan club

The soft sound of castanets drifted across the morning daybreak as effortlessly as a butterfly meandering over a garden in summer.

Except this was no summer day.

It was a cold, brisk December morning. A frost had settled overnight, not too thick to be troublesome, but thick enough to mean that car windscreens needed to be scraped with whatever device the driver had to hand. For Mitchell it was the back of an unused library card which he had found lurking in his wallet, not that he could actually remember signing up for one in the first place. No matter, it was coming in useful now.

Silently cursing, he stretched across his hire car and scratched at the frost. In his own car he knew he could slip into the drivers' seat, flick on the inbuilt heating system, sit back and wait for the frost to melt away. But he was undercover and needed to make do with the hire car his bosses had provided. An old, two bob, all-expense-spared rust bucket of a car. Not only had it seen better days, Mitchell thought that the car was probably around when the engine was first invented.

With that thought in mind, Mitchell chuckled to himself and put all the effort his little shortcrust frame could muster into shifting that last piece of frost. And as he reached out he never noticed the approaching figure from behind, syringe in one hand, castanets in the other.

****

He was awake now. A groggy conscious, but consciousness nonetheless.

He looked around trying to get his bearings. There was a stillness to the room with just the morning daylight streaking in through the skylights reflecting, glistening, off some tall metal units which seemed to adorn most of the walls. He closed his eyes and told himself to focus, his training for such events taking hold. Opening his eyes he was able to get a better sense of where he was being held.

A kitchen.

A sense of panic hit him causing bile to rush up his

throat. Swallowing hard he tried to move and realised he was tied down. A sudden sense of nakedness overwhelmed him as Mitchell felt cold steel touching his pale, shortcrust back. His aluminium tin coat had been removed, discarded on the floor next to where he was bound.

From the shadows appeared a tall, well-built male, dressed in a long white downy coat. His stature dominated the room and Mitchell found that he could not take his eyes of the impressive figure that had blended so elegantly into the darkness just a few moments beforehand.

"I am the last bastion of freedom, whereas you prefer to play the game of espionage." Although the tall figure spoke directly to Mitchell, it was as though he was talking to a wider audience.

"I know all about you. I have watched your every movement. You tried so hard to infiltrate my group, but to no avail. For I know you are a mince spy. A failed, pathetic mince spy who in a few short minutes will tell me what I want to know."

Mitchell watched the tall figure step back into the shadows, all the while hearing the rattle of castanets reverberate around the kitchen. He knew he needed to act fast in order to try to save himself and he valiantly fought against the straps which held down his arms and legs. With each movement, they dug deeper into his crust, the pain intensifying as mincemeat and spices began to seep out of his wounds. Mitchell stopped struggling and craned his neck forward to see what was holding him down. Freezer ties. Two per limb. He rested his head back against the cold metal to which he was tied. There was no escape.

The last bastion reappeared from the shadows, a childlike smile on his face. In his hands he held a long, plastic tube with a rubber top that was filled with what seemed to be a yellowish cream. With a few strides he stood before the mince spy, towering above his captive. He stooped low and eyeballed Mitchell, savouring the fear which shone through in his victim's eyes. He raised a surprisingly soft hand to Mitchell's face and gently caressed his latticed skin. With seemingly no effort, he gripped Mitchell's jaw and forced open his mouth inserting the plastic tube in one fluid motion. A short squeeze on the rubber nozzle and Mitchell felt the cream ooze into mouth, filling his throat and airways.

The taste was unmistakable.

He was going to drown in brandy butter.

And then, as he felt himself start to fade, the tube was removed and discarded to the floor next to his aluminium tin coat. Gasping for air, his lungs burning, Mitchell tried to refocus on the last bastion. He had taken a step back and was watching Mitchell closely.

"Now my dear mince spy, one question to save your life.

Who sent you?"

Mitchell knew that regardless of his answer he was not going to escape with his life. His years of training meant he took one final dignified stand and he refused to answer, taking this information to the grave.

The last bastion was not remotely surprised. He clicked his fingers and from deeper within the kitchen appeared two accomplices, one wearing a sombrero and one shaking the castanets which Mitchell had been hearing throughout this ordeal. Seeing a look of confusion cross Mitchell's face, the last bastion felt a warm glow rise inside of his body.

"Not many people realise that we originate from Mexico. You see that was your mistake too, and it has cost you your life."

The last bastion's two accomplices took hold of the metal structure to which Mitchell was strapped and flipped him so that he was facing the ceiling. They began to carry him further into the kitchen towards a glowing light that appeared to be hovering just above an open door.

It was then Mitchell realised he was being carried towards a fan oven.

And he was strapped to an oven griddle.

He fought for his life with the freezer ties ripping at his

crust, causing more mincemeat to spill from his body. The aroma of cinnamon, nutmeg and other spices, normally so appealing, would be the smell of his death.

With one final ironic insult, the last bastion stood above the mince spy, a brush dripping with egg wash aloft in his hand, which he swiped liberally across Mitchell's crust. The coldness of the egg wash sharpened Mitchell's senses alerting him to the fact that this liquid would only bring about his fate even more quickly.

And as he felt the heat from the oven prick at his latticed face, the last thing he saw was the temperature of the fan oven.

260 degrees.

It was of little solace that death for Mitchell the mince spy would be quick.

But, by Jove, death for him would be painful.

2

Snow White and seven dwarf cabbages

It was the scientific discovery that due to genetically modified food having greater volumes of nutrients, this meant the food started to develop the ability to think, breathe and talk on their own terms. The Genetically Modified Food Sapiens Act 1955, allowed food sapiens to be released from captivity and live, work and pay taxes alongside the homo sapiens community. While food sapiens hold above average intelligence and have been able to integrate into society, they have never worked out why there is a need to slap a lump of pineapple on top of a gammon steak.

Detective Inspector Willie Wortel, carrot, and head of the Food Related Crime team had seen many a disturbing scene in his time leading the specialised unit within the police force that focused on fighting crimes which occurred within the food sapiens community. Yet even with all of his experience, the latest news he was hearing had managed to shock him to his very core.

Alongside him when the revelations were being outlined was his trusted human colleague Dorothy Knox. And while Wortel was stunned by the news, Dorothy had streams of tears rolling down her face ruining the make-up she had taken so little time to apply that morning as she raced to work.

"I have to hear this again," said Wortel, his orange face losing some of its colour. "You are accusing Snow White of prostitution and being a drug taker?"

Oranges and Lemons, the two food sapiens officers that assisted, in the loosest possible sense, the Food Related Crime team, stared back at their boss wondering why he was having trouble absorbing their news.

"Boss, the evidence is overwhelming," implored Lemons. "She walks alone at night, finds a house, lets herself in and shacks up with seven men, in this case, seven dwarf cabbages. And the men know she offers tricks as well as being drugged up, we've told you."

Dorothy Knox let out another howl of laughter, her third in as many minutes. "Sing the song again, sing the song again," she screeched.

Oranges gave a pained expression to his partner Lemons. He too had no idea why this was proving so hard for his senior colleagues to understand.

"Well," sighed Wortel. "Go on; give us the song about the druggy prostitute Snow White."

Oranges and Lemons counted themselves in and, quite tunefully it must be said, launched into song.

"High Hoe, High Hoe,
High Hoe, High Hoe, off our face on meth we go!
With a shovel or a stick or a hashish kit!
High Hoe, High Hoe, High Hoe…"

Dorothy Knox roared once more and started banging her clenched hand on the table. "Stop it! Stop it! You're killing me…" she screamed, tears cascading down her face quicker than white water rapids.

For his part, DI Wortel just stood in stunned silence, amazed that these two fruit officers had managed to get through training and now, for his misfortune, were part of his team. And yet, when all was said and done, he had started to grow a little fond of them. In fact, he had even gone as far as recommending them for Taser training, although apparently, as Chief Superintendent Archibald had told him, it was against regulations to recommend officers to be shot with Tasers.

Wortel decided that he neither had the strength nor the inclination to tell Oranges and Lemons that they had been taken for a ride, yet again, by other members of the police force who were 'tipping them off with intelligence'. He turned to Dorothy who was slowly pulling herself together, while searching through her handbag for a dry tissue to replace the one which lay soaked on the side of her desk.

"Dotty, I've a meeting with the Chief at the Treasury offices, can you take these two misfruits through the pantomime version of Snow White. You know the version without the drug taking, the prostitution, the gangland hit on the wicked Queen."

"Oh, the dull version then?"

****

Wortel decided to take the stairs up to Chief Superintendent Archibald's office. It had been a crazy few months to say the very least, what with the surprise announcement from the Government Minister for the Department of Agriculture, Farming and Rural Trade (DAFaRT) that turkeys had been allowed to vote for or against Christmas, the result of which was due imminently; throw into the mix that because old age pensioners had been drag racing on their mobility scooters around town the speed limit had been cut to below 15mph; and that was without mentioning the murderous bananadrama, as the press had been calling the whole sorry affair.

Mind you, Wortel was pleased with the way the

bananadrama had been captured in Addicted to Death: A Food Related Crime Investigation – available to buy through Amazon at what he thought was the most reasonable of prices.

Who Killed The Mince Spy?

3

An offer you cannot refuse

Wortel and Archibald travelled together to the Treasury offices where an audience with Chancellor Stephen Green awaited. Waiting in the reception area Wortel began to fidget nervously as he thought about the previous time he was here when he discovered that passing security was a much more intimate experience than a simple pat down and a look inside any bags or briefcases.

"What's wrong with you Wortel?" asked Archibald becoming agitated by Wortel shifting from side to side.

"There's nothing wrong sir."

"Well then sit still for crying out loud. You're shifting about so much I'm starting to wonder if someone's lit a firecracker up your arse."

"I'm sorry sir. It's just, well, the last time I was here security was more thorough than I expected."

Chief Superintendent Archibald broke out into a broad grin. "Ah, I see. Yes, when I came here for the first time as a young whippersnapper I was a little taken aback when the rubber glove appeared."

"Rubber glove? Crikey, mine was a simple strip search," said Wortel.

Archibald looked surprisingly wistful. "They say the standards in this country are slipping Wortel. Seems the malaise has even infected the Treasury."

"So you don't think it's a little weird, you know, having to be, well, searched in that way?"

"Well, rest assured Wortel it won't happen today. I've top level security and I can vouch for you."

Wortel sighed in relief and settled back into the leather sofa which dominated the reception area. "Why has this meeting has been called sir?"

Archibald shrugged. "I'm as in the dark as you are Wortel. It wouldn't surprise me if Chancellor Green wanted to thank us in some way for all of the work around the bananadrama. After all, it's meant Green has been reinstated to the position of Chancellor."

Both man and carrot sat comfortably in the reception listening to the piped jazz tones of Fizzy Pop Gillespie as they waited to be taken up to meet with Chancellor Green. Eventually a well-meaning civil servant arrived to take them to their meeting, but before they could venture through the turnstile entrance, a recent new policy meant they needed health and safety training in order not to injure themselves on the impossibly slow moving contraption.

After a thirty-minute lecture, Wortel and Archibald were awarded a certificate meaning they were able to use the turnstile. However, Chief Superintendent Archibald had failed to notify the Treasury that Wortel was a carrot, and for this oversight Archibald clearly needed his equality training refreshed. A further hour slipped past while Archibald was indoctrinated in the new rules. Having promised never to have an original thought, he was allowed, with Wortel, to pass through the turnstile and forward to his meeting.

****

Chancellor Stephen Green was one of those people who it proved difficult to tell their age. His face looked weather-beaten and worn which gave the impression he was older than he really was. And in some ways that helped him as Chancellor, for it gave added weight and depth to what he said, even if the message was dressed up in the usual political language, otherwise known to the everyday man as piffle.

Archibald and Wortel were taken straight to Chancellor Green's office where they found him hands clamped behind his back, staring out of the window, his focus on the disused power station which stood on the banks of the Thames, crumbling brick by brick.

"Do you know," he said, not turning to face Archibald and Wortel, "that successive governments have said they intended to turn that building into something. It was going to be an arts centre, or an academy of science, or a sports facility for the poor, or fat, or the poor fat, something like that. And look, all this talk, and what's happened? Sweet bugger all, that's what's happened."

"Are you going to be the one to make change happen?" asked Wortel.

"Dear God no," laughed Green. "Can't be doing with any of that nonsense. Let someone else worry about it. I'm just here to make sure the books balance or when they don't, to make sure everyone knows it wasn't my fault."

Chancellor Green turned around and walked across to the two police officers. He stretched out his hand and shook Archibald's before turning to Wortel. He took Wortel by the hand and looked him up and down.

"Well, I have to say that after the Prime Minister sacked me I was living it up in Portugal on the golf courses. And then there was this food addiction scandal and Professor

Partridge gets killed. There is a public outcry and I'm back in post. I guess you know what I would like to say to you both don't you?"

Chief Superintendent Archibald stood proudly and patted Wortel on the shoulder. "We would say that we were only doing our job sir, but your thanks are most appreciated."

Green averted his eyes from Wortel and shifted his weight so that he was face to face with Archibald. "You seem to misunderstand me. I was doing fine on the golf course. My handicap was much improved and now I'm stuck back here looking after the country's finances, which frankly are shockingly bad, and I hate it."

Archibald felt his jaw dropping but managed to stop it before he gawped in front of the reinstated Chancellor. "But why did you come back then if you hate it so much?" asked Archibald, which was a perfectly reasonable question to ask.

"Professional pride. I do hate this work. But I tell you what I hated more. The fact the previous chap was better at it than I was. I would never have thought of taxing food and making it addictive. I would never have thought of allowing sponsorship deals for all major tourist attractions, events and famous people. He did. He might have been a rotter, but he was good at keeping this deficit under some form of control."

Wortel felt rather taken aback by what he was hearing. "Chancellor Green. So if I understand you correctly, you're coming back to try and do equally 'good' work?" Wortel could hear his own apprehension in his voice.

Chancellor Green threw back his head and roared with laughter. "My good carrot. No, like any good politician, I'm here to discredit him and then take the plaudits for his work."

It was Wortel's turn to feel his jaw start to drop. "So I guess it's safe to assume you are not going to repel the food tax then?"

"Not a chance. It is a money-spinner. The only difference is that I have no intention of getting into bed with a crooked CEO of a major food producer and committing murder."

"Ah, now sir, about that you do need to be careful what you say," said Archibald nervously. "We were never able to get any concrete evidence linking your predecessor to the murders, so he has never been charged on that point."

"Do you think you are going to find any evidence?" asked Green.

"Unlikely sir," replied Archibald, who had started to unscrew his false leg, his giveaway sign when he was nervous. "You see, the other people who we believe were part of the scam are all dead. So, it's hard to make them talk isn't it?"

"Yes it is. But actually, that's quite good news all things

considered."

Archibald and Wortel looked at each other and it was clear both man and carrot were utterly confused.

"How come sir?" pressed Archibald.

"Well you see the thing is, the Prime Minister has just started the general election campaign and there are only another 1,765 days to go. It wouldn't sit well if the government, and ministers of the government, were linked in some way to murder. That's why the Prime Minister has launched this independent enquiry into the food addiction scandal."

"Is that the independent enquiry which will be made up of self-appointed old cronies and which is already on its third chair person?" asked Wortel, feeling Archibald give him a sharp dig in the ribs.

"That'll be the one," replied Green cheerfully. "Anyway, it'll take at least two years before the enquiry eventually meets for the first time and then they'll need to agree terms of reference. That will go on for at least a year, and then once that's all sorted, well, I'm sure something will surface which will cause that chair and the cronies to stand down."

"And another few years will slip past with no outcome," offered Wortel, ignoring the jabbing in his ribs from his superior officer.

"You've got it in one Wortel. You're bright as a button. No wonder you have such a good record at the Food Related Crime team."

"How much is this going to cost the taxpayer?" said Wortel, taking two steps to his right to avoid Archibald who was making loud hushing noises.

"Far too much. It'll be well over budget. The sums will be eye watering, but no matter, justice will out. And the public will forget this whole affair ever happened in time. Let's be honest, they forgave the Chancellor before me for selling off the gold reserves of the country for a packet of fruit pastilles."

Wortel shrugged in defeated acceptance. "One final question sir, if I may?"

"Of course you may."

"Why are we here?"

Chancellor Green smiled. "I would like to make you an offer that I don't think you can refuse."

Wortel felt his back stiffen at the suggestion, while Chief Superintendent Archibald, who had unscrewed, and then re-screwed his leg, looked at Chancellor Green with intrigue.

Chancellor Green noticed how he caught the attention

of Chief Superintendent Archibald and moved into the space which Wortel had vacated when his boss was jabbing him in the ribs. Chancellor Green placed his arm around Archibald's shoulder and turned him away from Wortel.

"I can only imagine how expensive it is to run your division Chief Superintendent Archibald."

"Oh it is sir. We are always looking for ways to save money aren't we Wortel?"

Wortel went to reply but Chancellor Green beat him to the punch.

"I thought as much. Which is why I want to increase the funding for your team. I want to make sure you have funds to cover your expenses for the lifetime of this parliament."

"How generous of you," boomed Archibald, taking Chancellor Green by the hand and shaking it vigorously.

Chancellor Green pulled his hand away sharply, causing Archibald to stumble slightly. Obviously he hadn't tightened his false leg as well as he had thought.

"Just one thing Archibald. One small condition."

'Here it comes' thought Wortel.

"I need to be confident that this murder case isn't going to come and bite me on the backside. So do I have your word Chief Superintendent Archibald?"

Chief Superintendent Archibald mulled over the offer for a matter of seconds. "So when do we get the increased funds?"

Wortel threw his arms up in the air and bought them down on top of his head. Archibald looked in his direction and smiled weakly. "Look on the bright side. This means you get to keep Oranges and Lemons for so much longer."

Chancellor Green walked Archibald and Wortel to the lifts and wished them well before departing. He liked them. He liked the way Archibald did business. And he liked the way Wortel wasn't afraid of showing his emotions. Especially how he had burst into tears on realising he was able to keep his team together.

****

It was in the taxi on the way back to the office that Wortel managed to regain his composure and stop the flood of tears. Putting his handkerchief back into trouser pocket, Wortel took a long sniff, shook his head and followed that up with a deep sigh.

Archibald, who had become increasingly embarrassed by his colleague's behaviour and had been pretending he wasn't with Wortel, stopped staring out of the taxi window and turned to Wortel.

"Have you quite finished?"

"Yes, I'm sorry about that sir," said Wortel who felt he would burst into tears again if Archibald pressed him too hard.

"Thank the lord. You really embarrassed me in front of the Chancellor."

"I was overcome sir. The thought of another five years with Oranges and Lemons, well, it was too much for me. You'd be the same if you were with them every second of the working day."

"I would have held myself together; I can tell you that for nothing Wortel. I was mortified as we walked through reception with you blubbing like there was no tomorrow. The shame of it."

"And I suppose you falling over because you hadn't reattached your false leg properly had nothing to do with your embarrassment at all," replied Wortel more tartly than he wanted.

Archibald reddened in the face as he remembered going arse upwards. "I think I slipped on the wet floor which had arisen because of your tears," he shot back.

"I very much doubt that," replied Wortel. "Anyway, I thought the receptionist was very gracious about the whole thing, especially as your leg hit her on the temple and smashed her glasses."

Archibald turned away from Wortel and began to stare out of the window again, with neither man nor carrot speaking for the remainder of the journey.

****

Dorothy consoled Wortel on his arrival back at the Food Related Crime offices.

"Want to hear something amusing?" she asked.

"Do I ever?"

"I told Oranges and Lemons the real story of Snow White and suffice to say they were a bit disappointed. Anyway, they initially misheard me and thought I was talking about how to communicate with deaf pandas, but I made them realise I was saying pantomime…"

Wortel raised his eyes to the ceiling.

"…well, they got quite excited by the idea of performing on stage and they've booked themselves in for some auditions. We might be off to see them in a panto this year."

The news did indeed bring a smile to Wortel's face as he slipped off his overcoat and hung it up on the coat rack.

"What pantomime?" Wortel asked tentatively.

Dorothy let out a small giggle. "I'm not entirely sure but I just know I stopped them from auditioning from a risky 'adults' only panto – A-lad-in Dick Whittington."

Who Killed The Mince Spy?

4

Pluck-It

The cameras were positioned. The studio lights set. Settee at the ready, cushions plumped. The stage hand signalled to the highly experienced, but somewhat temperamental anchor, at least that's what it sounded like they called him, that they were to go live in 5…4…3…2…1…

"And good evening everybody, welcome to this live edition of NewsFoodNight, during which we shall learn which way the turkeys have voted. Will they have voted for or against Christmas? The opinion polls have this as a vote too close to call and the ramifications of this vote shall live on for a generation. Are we consigned to eating nut cutlets before our Christmas pudding or can we carry on with our traditional Christmas turkey dinner? With me tonight to answer these questions and to discuss the results will be the fool who allowed this referendum to take place, the Minister for DAFaRT, and the maniac/genius you choose, who secured this referendum, Chief Turkey Gobbler Tarquinius Gallopava."

Off set the television crew watched the host of NewsFoodNight, Paxo, whip himself up into a frenzy in readiness for his first victim Sir Rupert Irksome, Minister for DAFaRT. Paxo was a fearsome interviewer and although small in stature he lived up to his food sapiens nickname Paxo the Stuffing. Perched on the end of his Pyrex dish seat, he would lull in his guests with his softly spoken sage words, before unleashing an onion-based tongue lashing if he felt they were not being straight with their answers. Many a time Ned St.NoBalls, the leader of the opposition party WeKipped, had appeared opposite Paxo and was carried off set a quivering wreck. In one ill-fated confrontation, Ned St.NoBalls had decided to march on stage shouting 'hell yeah', only to find that Paxo was asking aloud a question about whether people thought the WeKipped economic policy of funding research into growing money on trees was preposterous. Such was the PR disaster that WeKipped advised him to sit on the floor of a moving bus, ignoring all of the empty seats, and make a claim that he was on medication which was causing him to act strangely.

Sir Rupert made his way onto the television studio floor, shook hands with Paxo the Stuffing and settled down for his grilling.

"If I may cut to the chase?" asked Paxo.

Sir Rupert nodded.

"Of all the food groups, what possessed you to offer the turkeys, the vote on Christmas? Were you out of your simple little mind?"

Sir Rupert expected such an opening question and took the insult in his stride by sticking up his middle finger and saluting Paxo, who for his part, thumbed his nose right back at Sir Rupert.

"A very sage question," said Sir Rupert, hoping to get a laugh from the audience. The only trouble for Sir Rupert was that there was no audience in the studio and opposite him sat Paxo the Stuffing who was browning in the face at the comment.

Sir Rupert decided to press on. "In fact Paxo, I have no idea why I offered the referendum. I accept that I did as my signature is all over the parliamentary papers and I ordered the press release announcing the date of the referendum. As for why I did, I couldn't honestly say. I actually have no recollection of the whole affair. All I can remember is that I had a much bruised arm like I had given blood but I felt an extreme contentment. Strange isn't it?"

It wasn't often that you saw Paxo lost for words, although this was becoming one such occasion.

"So, if you don't recall the reason for the referendum, what does Prime Minister Greggs have to say?"

"He's told me that he's buggered if he is going to have his name dragged through the mud on this one and so if the turkeys vote against Christmas then I will need to resign. Your arse not my arse, I think were his words."

"But why hasn't he called this referendum off? Surely there are good grounds to do so?"

"No, no. He has party unity in mind you see?"

Off stage an advisor to Sir Rupert was doing his best to attract his attention to get him to stop talking. He stood waving his arms frantically in the air, in one hand a mobile phone with a connection to the Prime Minister's office who were screaming blue murder down the line.

"Party unity?" Paxo realised he had TV gold and sometimes the best thing was to not ask long questions but to let the interviewee talk themselves into a hole.

"Yes. We in Unions-R-Us pride ourselves on not having party unity for too long. The Prime Minister was looking for some mechanism for the party to rip itself apart and this came along."

"But how can that be good for government and the country?"

"It isn't Paxo, you old fool. While the party is tearing itself to pieces and the wheels of government come to a grinding halt, the Prime Minister and his old school cronies can line their pockets with expenses and off the book contracts. Look at the recent honours announcement. There was a dame-hood for the lady who works in the PM's chip shop. We've heard she slips him an extra big portion and a pork saveloy from time to time and there's her reward. It's been happening for years."

Off stage the advisor to Sir Rupert had decided that desperate times called for desperate measures and with no other option, they hit the nearest fire alarm. Running onto set they grabbed a startled Sir Rupert by the lapels and started to drag him away from Paxo the Stuffing.

"Bad show about the fire alarm," said Sir Rupert to his advisor, "…I thought that was going swimmingly."

****

With the fire evacuation over and Sir Rupert bundled into a car heading for Coventry, Paxo the Stuffing was back with breaking news.

"Ladies and Gentlemen of the United Kingdom. Homo sapiens and food sapiens alike. The results are in, and I can now reveal that the turkeys have, by record numbers, voted against Christmas. A landslide 72% voted with Chief Turkey Gobbler Tarquinius Gallopava, just 22% against, with the remaining 6% having spoiled their ballot papers by eating them. So there we have it, it wasn't remotely close and the opinion polls were wrong again, tripe in fact, with respect to that rather awful food sapiens group. The government have suffered more than just a bloody nose tonight and the good people of the UK will be no longer able to enjoy a traditional Christmas roast dinner. Sharing his thoughts on this momentous result is Chief Turkey Gobbler himself, Tarquinius Gallopava."

Strutting onto stage with long strides, Tarquinius Gallopava craned his thin neck as high as it would go, puffing out his tail feathers for all to see. Here was a turkey who was going to make the most of his victory and everybody was going to know about it.

Paxo the Stuffing watched this triumphant white-feathered bird reach the interview sofa, cluck backwards and forwards for a short while, turn around a couple of times, his head bobbing backwards and forwards, before he plonked his large frame down and indicated he was ready to begin.

"A fairly clear victory in the end wasn't it?" said Paxo, not trying to hide the sneer in his voice.

"Never in doubt. And I am pleased to say that your sort will never be stuffed near a turkey's giblets again. Let us be clear, turkeys have voted against our continuing exploitation. We are a free species."

"You always were a free species," snapped Paxo. "What you have done is to campaign on the fears of turkeys around the UK by claiming they would never be part of a Sunday roast again. That isn't true?"

"That's not what I said."

"But you did. Your campaign trail specifically said 'we boast, no to the roast'. Are you now saying, with the result confirmed, that you only meant the Christmas roast and not all Sunday roasts? I put it to you that your campaign was disingenuous."

"I am sorry if people misunderstood the nature of the campaign, although I know all turkeys that voted with me clearly grasped this concept. As for that slogan, it was not part of my official 'no' campaign."

"You lied."

"Not so. I campaigned against turkeys being the staple for the Christmas dinner and this was overwhelmingly backed by the majority of turkeys. They have gobbled and we respect that result."

"What do you make of the Minister for DAFaRT claiming he cannot remember why he called this referendum?"

"The Minister made his reasons clear in his press release all those months ago. He valued our choice of freedom which we have today taken. Other than that, I have no comment to make. The Minister can speak for himself."

"So are you satisfied with the campaign you ran?"

"I worked this campaign hard. I had a number of events around the country and I gobble, gobbled here, gobble, gobbled there…"

"…here a gobble," injected Paxo.

"…yes, there a gobble…"

"…everywhere a gobble, gobble…"

"Indeed," said Tarquinius. "I don't think I need to go on any further."

****

With a press of a button the television was paused, Tarquinius Gallopava frozen in time, his plume of feathers filling the screen, his red long neck protruding from his body.

The rotund gentleman watching NewsFoodNight drained the last remnants of scotch from his glass before he stood from his chair. On his wall was a map of the world, across which arrows were drawn in what appeared to be a random order but yet which made complete sense to him. He stroked his beard, his eyes fixated on the Chief Turkey Gobbler.

"I don't like you one bit. You need to be watched very carefully my friend," he said aloud.

"What was that dear?" his wife called from the adjacent room.

"Oh just mumbling to myself," he called back, before using the remote again to turn off the television.

"First sign of madness Nicholas," she replied. "Careful or I will call the little men in green coats."

"Ho, Ho, Ho," Nicholas chuckled as he walked across to a small handmade wooden cabinet which was fixed to the wall. He opened the cabinet door, looked at the contents inside and withdrew a long, sharp-pointed syringe.

5

Ten Lords a leaping; Nine Ladies dancing...

Wortel and the team arrived at Goodeatery, the restaurant of Scottie Rodgers the famous celebrity chef. The call to the Food Related Crime team had been made earlier by a member of the restaurant cleaning staff – they had a found a body.

The journey had been one which Wortel was trying to forget mainly because Oranges and Lemons had spent most of the time asking if they were there yet, while Dorothy was blathering on about it being a sure sign Christmas was coming, because apparently the upper classes had started acting strangely as they do at this time of year, what with the lords leaping and ladies dancing among other things. And then when he turned on the car radio all they were talking about was the result of the turkey referendum and the disclosure that Ned

St.NoBalls had issued a statement saying he was only 7½ in favour of a turkey dinner anyway.

A police commissioned double-decker bus pulled up at the scene and from the rear entrance alighted the medical examiner Dr Richards, her overly large head being the first thing that caught Dorothy's attention, which was far from surprising as most people tended to take a second, and sometimes, third glance when Dr Richards first appeared. Dr Richards was carrying her medical bag and as she departed the police bus she called out a cheery farewell to the conductor. She spotted Dorothy and waved before heading into Goodeatery. Dorothy gave a wave back and admired the way Dr Richards was able to ignore the gasps and stares from onlookers. There were only two occasions when Dorothy knew Dr Richards was conscious about the size of her head. Once during the recent egg beating case when an allergic reaction caused her head to swell to an even larger size, and once when she wore a red hat and while walking down the road, traffic mistook her for a stop sign. She had struggled for some time to get over the embarrassment of the four-mile tailback that had occurred.

The scene inside of Goodeatery was one of the most horrific the Food Related Crime team had faced, with the burnt body of Mitchell the mince spy, trapped within a fan oven. While his charred features were barely recognisable, it was clear he had been tied to the griddle and that his face, or what remained of his face, was looking out towards whoever had placed him inside the oven.

Dr Richards had the unenviable task of removing Mitchell from the oven.

"Morning everyone," she said not lifting her big moon face from the corpse, which was a relief to them all, as she could have easily sent them scattering like skittles across the crime scene.

She continued apace. "Seems to me like we have some sort of pie here. Although my autopsy will confirm what type, I suspect it is a mince pie what with the aroma."

Everyone hated to admit it at a crime scene, but even though he was badly burnt, now that the oven door had been opened he smelt divine.

"I cannot determine a time of death yet but the cause is clear. I will try to be more accurate when I have him back on the slab. And for the record Wortel, the fan oven was turned off when we arrived. The cleaner told me they never touched the scene, so your murderer, and let's be clear this is not death by misadventure, watched the mince pie die and then turned the oven off."

As Wortel and Dorothy absorbed that rather disturbing fact, Oranges and Lemons giggled that Dr Richards had said 'mince pie die' and therefore she was a poet but did not know it.

"And what are you two giggling about?" enquired Wortel, far from impressed at their crime scene conduct.

Both Oranges and Lemons shook their head and never answered although they did a pantomime style thigh slap for good measure.

"Slap your thigh again and I'll slap your head," Wortel warned them.

"Abusing a fellow officer, that won't do at all," Dorothy teased him.

"Can you blame me?"

"No, not really. Look boys, come here."

Oranges and Lemons trotted over to Dorothy who asked them to make a list of kitchen staff members and their current whereabouts. A look of seriousness came across their faces as they went about their business. Either that or they both had constipation.

Wortel and Dorothy walked through the Goodeatery kitchen looking for anything that might be evidence in the murder which they were now investigating. Across the kitchen floor Dorothy spotted the aluminium coat which Mitchell had been wearing. Catching Wortel's attention she pointed to where the coat lay. Wortel nodded and let out a snort.

"What was that for?" she asked.

"Just an ironic little twist, I suppose. Only right there was where Scottie Rodgers and I had to defuse the chocolate bomb cake."

"Really?"

"Yes, I can tell because it's next to the station of Sue Chef the Sous Chef, but between the station of the Soup Chef and the Suet Chef."

"Oh yes," replied Dorothy, eyes rolling to the ceiling. "I seem to recall you mentioning that once or twice before."

It had only been a few months earlier that Wortel had found himself at Goodeatery with the celebrity chef Scottie Rodgers, running bravely into danger to rescue Donatella DiMaggio, another celebrity chef, who had been kidnapped and tied up in the store room. They managed to defuse a chocolate bomb cake with just seconds to spare using only some noodles, a spatula and a can of whipped cream. The event resulted in Donatella DiMaggio and Scottie Rodgers beginning a torrid love affair from which he had not yet recovered. To say she was too much for him was an understatement and he was in hospital with severe back problems receiving daily physiotherapy.

Dorothy took some photographs of the scene and having slipped on some latex gloves, she moved the aluminium coat of Mitchell the mince spy. Slipping her hand into his inside pocket she withdrew a wallet that contained a driving licence where a smiling Mitchell looked back at her. She handed it to Wortel who was busy bagging up a long tube with a rubber top that was partly filled with a yellowish substance.

"Do you know what this is?" he asked her.

Dorothy looked at the instrument and blushed.

"What did I say?" he exclaimed

"Nothing. Just reminded me of an article I read once about pregnancy. Anyway, I think it's a baster but what that yellowy stuff is I don't know."

Wortel eyed Dorothy up suspiciously and made

a mental note to run an internet search later on pregnancy in kitchens. As the cogs in his mind whirled, Oranges and Lemons came over to their two senior officers.

"We'll have the names of all the workers within the next two hours boss as well as their home addresses. We've also asked for surrounding CCTV footage to be sent to the office so we can review it," said Oranges.

Wortel was surprised by their diligence. This was most unlike the two fruit officers.

"Well done boys," he said. "Congratulations for thinking about the CCTV."

"Well it was Dr Richards really," spoke Lemons not engaging his brain as usual. "It was her suggestion."

Wortel and Dorothy exchanged a look while Oranges dug his partner firmly in the ribs with a well-timed elbow.

"Sorry boss," said Lemons, his eyes now fixated at the ground. "Only I forget what we should be doing. Some of the restaurant workers arrived and they started going on about obese poultry and I got confused."

Feeling his shoulders start to tighten, Wortel swallowed hard and braced himself.

"Obese poultry?" he asked.

"Yes, the workers were saying Christmas is coming and the geese are getting fat. Boss, they did raise some questions?"

"What?"

"Who is the old man and why do we need to put a penny in his hat?"

6

Hey diddle, diddle, a Widdle store card fiddle

She looked in the long mirror which hung in her bedroom.

Perfect.

Bright red lipstick. Flowing dress. Killer heels.

She was ready for the night's work.

****

The night was closing in and the cold December air pricked at their faces as they left their house.

The group hurried towards their car knowing that in a short while she would be standing on the street corner waiting for them.

It was almost pick-up time.

****

He was drunk.

No two ways about it.

Drunk as a skunk.

Again.

****

She headed out into the night and wished she had picked up a coat.

She tugged at the bolero that hung around her shoulders. It was the wrong thing to be wearing at this time of the year.

Still, she knew that she would be getting into a car in the not too distant future and that thought kept the cold at bay.

****

"Oh, he won't like you getting into the vehicle

drunk," he said aloud to himself. "Well, he can go and jump off a cliff for all I care."

He looked down at the bottles which littered the floor. He had stolen his masters store card of Widdle, low cost shopping centre for the incontinent, and gone on an alcoholic spending spree.

He staggered towards the vehicle, opened the door and after a few attempts, managed to get the key into the ignition.

"Thank god I don't have to pull this thing anymore," he said to the empty street which lay ahead of him.

****

"How much longer until we reach her, I'm terribly cramped in the back here?"

"Will you give it a rest, you grumpy old sod?" came a dopey reply from the front.

"Aitchoo," responded another.

****

"He likes the others better than me, the fat old bastard. Says he doesn't but I know differently," he slurred.

The vehicle was gathering speed and was swaying from one side of the road to the other.

"Let's go to the ballet again so we can see good old dancer and prancer…nobody remembers them anyway."

****

She looked at her watch. They were late. And the cold air had started to pierce through to her bones.

Having reached the agreed street corner, she leant up against the lamppost and decided that she was going to take a swig from a secret flask which she carried attached discreetly to her thigh. Warm apple cider. Delicious.

Looking around, she saw in the distance a vehicle turn the corner rather too quickly.

Deciding she had time to take a sip from the flask, she leaned forward and hitched up her skirt.

****

"I don't want her to see me when she gets into the car," the petite little chap said shyly as their vehicle turned into the street where they would pick her up.

****

The swaying vehicle was violently out of control as it hurtled down one street and then another, his steering more frantic than ever.

"I'm Rudolph the red-nosed reindeer
I have a very shiny nose
And if you ever saw it
I'd say stop looking at me I just want to be a normal reindeer like the others…"

He laughed out loud at his own inventiveness, not seeing the young lady, skirt in the air, leg showing, standing on the street corner.

****

The driver of six petite dwarf cabbages approached the pick-up point.

He could see Snow White standing on the street corner ready for the night's action. And he could also see a motorised sleigh heading straight for her.

If only he didn't feel so tired he might be able to do something about it.

****

Hearing what sounded like a reindeer singing a rather crude song, Snow White looked up and saw the out of control sleigh heading right for her as she stood on the street corner. She looked in the opposite direction and saw the car carrying the dwarf cabbages drift in her direction too.

"Ah, bollocks," said Snow White, in her thick Geordie accent. "They've only let Sleepy drive again."

****

The Food Related Crime team arrived at the scene shortly after the call was received and they began their examination of the head on collision.

Oranges and Lemons had come dressed as pantomime dames in preparation for their audition the next day, while Wortel was sporting a pain his arm which was a result of suggesting to Dorothy that she should take make-up tips from the two fruit officers.

Snow White was being carried into the back of a waiting ambulance; Rudolph was being cut from the wreckage of the sleigh not because he was badly injured but because his antler had become trapped in the airbag which had inflated on impact.

Wortel turned to the six dwarf cabbages who had

somehow escaped with only minor bruising, although the odour they omitted was rather more disturbing.

"How come there are only six of you?" he asked them.

Doc stepped forward. "We'd arranged to meet the other one at the theatre in advance of this evening's pantomime rehearsal. I've just got off the phone to him."

"How did he take the news?" enquired Wortel.

"He wasn't happy."

Who Killed The Mince Spy?

7

The prunes with the runes

It is difficult to describe that strange sensation, that feeling you sometimes get in the pit of your stomach, when you just know something is wrong. Wortel had that feeling. It was there when he awoke. It stayed with him while he showered. It never left as he had breakfast, all the while dodging his son Jack's attempts to hit him with spoonfuls of muesli that he didn't want to eat – not that Wortel blamed him. As he drove to work the feeling began to intensify. Something was amiss.

He ran through the events of last night.

Snow White was in hospital with a couple of cracked ribs, a cut to her head and a fat lip. When he called the hospital this morning they had said there was nothing to be concerned about as she would soon be the fairest of them all again in around four to six weeks. Five of the six dwarf cabbages were allowed back home while Sleepy was arrested for dangerous driving.

Rudolph was sleeping it off in a cell back at the station, and between rude Christmas songs he was being given lots of black coffee. Apparently his latest ditty had proven to be quite popular at the station and was doing the rounds. Much to Wortel's surprise he too was humming it as he drove to work.

"Chests and Nuts roasting on an open fire
Nudists please put on some clothes
'cos things could get rather dire
At your age, dangly bits hang down to your toes."

Arriving at work he visited the canteen, purchased his morning coffee and took a sip. Nope. That didn't make him feel any better. And when he saw Dorothy loitering outside the Food Related Crime office with a stern look upon her face he could feel the knot in his stomach tighten even more.

"Morning Dorothy. What's wrong?"

"Morning boss. Now why would anything be wrong?"

"Because you never wait in the corridor pretending to do yoga stretches. So, what's wrong?"

"Now, promise you won't get mad."

"That depends. Why would I get mad?"

"Just promise. And try to keep in mind that Chief Superintendent Archibald is only trying to help."

Wortel felt his shoulders sag and his legs get suddenly heavier. He looked at Dorothy who stood down from her praying mantis pose and return her left leg back to the floor. She shrugged and stood aside so that Wortel could enter the office.

The first thing Wortel noticed as he opened the door wasn't that the room had been completely rearranged. It wasn't that the lights had been turned off and that there was a soft dim radiating from a number of candles strategically placed around the room. It wasn't even the background music which was a mix between whale noises and monk chanting. Mind you, it could easily have been monk noises and whales chanting, it was difficult to say with any certainty. No, the thing which Wortel noticed first was the smell.

You see the thing with food sapiens is that they have an enhanced sense of smell. That's why the famous singer Curly Kale Minogue is often seen gagging on stage. It's not through nerves as her publicity states, but because often concert-goers, and particularly those who get front row tickets, happen to be members of the great unwashed and the smell from them can be overwhelming.

Wortel, somewhat unwisely, took in a large breath. Incense. Well, to be honest he was hopping mad actually, but it was the smell of incense which launched an all-out assault on his nostrils. That soon shifted the knot in his stomach, although he felt it was pushing something far worse up his gullet that might result in a projectile incident.

Swallowing hard, Wortel regained his composure. He felt Dorothy place her hand on his shoulder where she gave a short squeeze. He appreciated her concern and smiled inwardly. Looking around the office he saw Chief Superintendent Archibald, Oranges and Lemons and two small, shrivelled things sitting on the floor in a circle. Well, not directly on the floor, but perched precariously on beanbags.

Wortel looked at Dorothy and could sense that his face was telling a thousand words. She looked back at him and with a tilt of her head she seemed to acknowledge that she could feel his pain.

"Do I have to do this?" he whispered out of the side of his mouth.

"If I am going in, then so are you," she replied in equally hushed tones.

"Well, once more into the breach then."

"Together as always."

Wortel took another deep breath and regretted it immediately as the incense burned at the back of his throat. He started to splutter causing Dorothy to slap him firmly on the back as he tried to regain some semblance of control.

"Thanks," he gasped. "What would I do without you?"

"You'd have to train Oranges and Lemons up to my standards," she replied not trying to conceal the hint of irony in her voice.

Before Wortel had the chance to respond, which was probably going to consist of a significant amount of swearing, Chief Superintendent Archibald called across the rearranged Food Related Crime office.

"Ah, Wortel, do come on over and meet these two guests that I have invited to help with the investigation."

"Sir," said Wortel on reaching the beanbag circle and seeing Oranges and Lemons sitting comfortably both with red scarves wrapped around their heads. "May I have a word in private?"

"No can do, I'm afraid Wortel," replied Archibald who was wearing a rather fetching large brown belt with an oversized metal buckle. It went well with the white pirate shirt he was wearing especially for the occasion.

"Well, don't just stand there. Take a seat and then I can introduce everyone." Archibald waved his hand towards the empty beanbags and chose to ignore Wortel as he rolled his eyes despairingly. "Oh, and grab a garment, everyone must wear something."

Dorothy moved quicker than Wortel and plopped to the

floor while grabbing the single remaining red scarf which lay discarded in the middle of the circle. Wortel lowered himself towards the floor and let out an audible sigh as he leaned forward and picked up the gold-coloured turban which Dorothy had skilfully avoided. He rested the turban on his head and hearing Dorothy start to snigger, tugged at her beanbag causing her to topple sideways and sprawl unladylike over the floor.

Archibald glared across at his two supposedly senior staff members and made a loud, fake cough in order to get everyone's attention. "Thank you all for being here," he began.

"Where else would we be, it's our bloody office?" remarked Wortel cattily to Dorothy who had now managed to get her arse back onto a beanbag and not from pointing at the ceiling.

"I have invited two distinguished guests to help with the investigation. I realise we have only just processed the crime scene and our burnt to a crisp mince pie is with Dr Richards, but every little help counts," Archibald said talking louder so as to drown out the backchat from Wortel. "Please welcome two prunes who use runes."

The silence which enveloped the room was such that any passer-by to the Food Related Crime office might have mistaken the event for a minute's silence in memory of a fallen colleague. Slowly, tentatively even, Lemons raised his hand.

"Yes Lemons, what is it?" asked Archibald, pleased that someone was at last taking an interest.

"Forgive me for asking sir, but you tried something like this in our previous investigation with the bananadrama. We had psychometric rhubarb last time, and well, not wanting to be rude, but it was rubbish."

Dorothy attempted to prevent her laughter from being too obvious by shoving a loose piece of red cloth that was draped around her head, firmly into her mouth. Wortel himself felt a guffaw building and tried to turn it into a spluttering fit similar to what he had when he felt he had swallowed half a ton of incense.

Archibald stroked his chin and thought of the best way to respond. "Well, I admit that my last attempt to help may not have proved as successful as I had hoped. But I would say that on the up side, it showed we need to think beyond the traditional methods and explore some untraditional methods. This is why we are exploring divination at this session."

Lemons face struck its usual confused look. He turned to Oranges who was trying to give the appearance of sitting serenely on the beanbag when in reality he was clenching hard with his buttocks so not to fall sideways.

"Oranges. Why are we meeting to talk about stupid countries?"

"Pardon?" exclaimed Oranges nearly unclenching and losing balance.

"Chief Superintendent Archibald has said we are going to talk about stupid countries. He said it himself, divi nations."

Oranges turned his head, lost control of his buttocks and sprawled forward into Lemons who also went flying. From his newly found prone position, Oranges started to scold his fruit partner.

"No you fool. Archibald said divination. There's a difference," muttered Oranges sharply, while carefully placing his cheeks back onto the beanbag and getting ready to re-clench.

"Really? I never knew. So what's this divination malarkey then?" replied Lemons picking himself up and adjusting his scarf.

Oranges, realising he didn't actually know what divination was, chose to ignore the question and mumbled a response about how he should be quiet and maybe he would learn something.

Archibald, who knew he had lost control of the situation, fake coughed again and passed the floor to the two wrinkly looking prunes that were decked from head to toe in green and blue flowing garments more suited to a fancy dress shop than a serious police department. Well, maybe describing the Food Related Crime team as a serious department is an overstatement, but the garb seemed far from appropriate.

Wrinkly prune number one spoke first with a somewhat indistinguishable accent which Wortel and Dorothy would later describe over the water cooler as 'French-cum-Thames estuary'.

"Mesdames et messieurs, and er, well foodies I guess, thanks a million for inviting ze great Prunes a la Runes to assist with your stalling investigation."

Wortel looked aghast and glared at Chief Superintendent Archibald who himself had become fixated on a small spider he had spotted walking across the ceiling. He turned to Dorothy. "Stalling investigation. We've not had the chance to start it yet."

The wrinkly prune number two, whose accent was much more refined, continued. "We can help provide you with a breakthrough clue, but first we need to identify which of the group is most attuned with the rune world."

To say the Food Related Crime team sat forward in anticipation would be, frankly, a whopper of epic proportions.

"So, I need everybody to say out loud a rune number, between one and ten. You first," wrinkly prune number two said pointing a withered looking finger at Chief Superintendent Archibald.

Archibald sat in silence for what felt like an eternity as he weighed up his options. Finally, as though he had received an epiphany, he spoke. "Rune number three."

Wrinkly prune number one shook his head and pointed towards Oranges.

"Rune number one."

"No. You."

Lemons looked suspiciously at the wrinkly prune before whispering "rune number two".

Wrinkly prune number one shook his head disappointedly while Lemons punched the air in delight.

Wortel could feel his stomach starting to knot once more. As the wrinkly prune looked in his direction he took a breath and said "rune number nine".

Wrinkly prune number one reached behind where he was sitting and pulled forward a bag containing something rather heavy. He reached inside and clasped his hand around the object before closing his eyes and going into a deep think. A full two minutes of complete silence passed before he opened his eyes and smiled a gummy grin at Wortel.

"No. Next."

Wortel sat upright so quickly his gold turban very nearly flew from his head. He'd escaped! Dorothy not waiting to be asked sat forward.

"Finally," she said aloud. "Didn't think I was going to get a go. Rune number eight."

Both wrinkly prunes looked at each other and started to nod vigorously. "Oh yes," wrinkly prune number two cried. "You're the one."

The two prunes with the runes invited Dorothy to join them in the middle of the circle so she was face to face with them. She tried leaping to her feet quickly which just resulted in her ending up once more sprawled face down and legs akimbo. Once she had managed to get into position, with the help of Oranges and Lemons who heaved her back to her feet, the wrinkly prunes were ready to continue.

Wrinkly prune number one. "What zis your name?"

"Dorothy."

"Ah. A great English name full of ze style and ze grace."

Archibald started to chuckle given Dorothy had looked anything but just a few moments ago.

Wrinkly prune number two took over. "We have been

given an outline of your case. But in order to help us, please give us three numbers of your choosing between one and a hundred."

Dorothy smiled at the two wrinkly prunes. "That's very easy. My numbers are 36-28-34. Can you guess what those figures relate to?"

"Your imagination," called out Wortel causing the office to erupt in laughter.

Dorothy did not look across at Wortel but flicked him a two-fingered salute, which caused the laughter to continue for longer.

The two prunes went into deep deliberation before a calm serenity appeared on their faces. Wrinkly prune number two spoke.

"Your numbers have been enlightening. They have provided us with a clear picture and we are sure a breakthrough clue."

"Go on," urged Dorothy.

"We see a building. It is calm, still. No, that is wrong, It is cold. But there is danger. We can see you actually, and you are running, but we are not sure if it towards or away from something."

"Me. Running!" exclaimed Dorothy.

"It zurprised us too," said wrinkly prune number one rather too quickly for Dorothy's liking.

"Yes, you are running. But then it goes black and we cannot see much more. Your last rune is interesting."

"In what way," asked Dorothy now intrigued.

"Do you like buttercups?"

"I prefer roses but I don't mind them. Why?"

"It is too difficult to tell. I sense that is important though."

"How interesting," said Dorothy not really sure if it was interesting at all.

Wortel had reached the end of his tether, in part because he had work he needed to do like to discover who the dead mince pie was, but mainly because he was getting a numb backside from the really quite uncomfortable beanbag.

"Sir," he said looking across to Chief Superintendent Archibald. "We really do need to be getting on with the investigation."

"We are done here anyway," said wrinkly prune number two. "Our invoice will be in the post Chief Superintendent."

Who Killed The Mince Spy?

8

MI GasMark5

Now that the prunes with the runes had left the building, Wortel and his team were able to rearrange their office and get started with the murder investigation.

"What do you think they meant by asking what flowers I liked?" asked Dorothy, as she and Wortel picked up the final out of place desk and carried back across the office floor.

"No idea," replied Wortel. "I wouldn't worry about it too much."

Oranges and Lemons were both looking at the same computer screen, staring intently at the message which kept appearing.

"Do it again Oranges," urged Lemons, as his fruit officer partner became more agitated at the computer.

Oranges began tapping at his keyboard before throwing his arms up in the air once more. Dorothy sensed Wortel's anxiety and intimated that she would go and see what they were up to. As she walked across to them, Chief Superintendent Archibald came limping back into the office.

Wortel smiled at his boss and deciding against mentioning the prunes with the runes.

"How is Mrs Archibald?" asked Wortel through his ridiculous sense of duty rather than any actual care in the world.

"Oh, very busy Wortel, very busy indeed. There was a television appeal recently for knitting clubs all over the country to start 'knitting one, pearling one', to help the poor livestock who get very cold at Christmas time. Well, Mrs A was on it like a flash and as Christmas approaches Wortel, I'm so proud to say Mrs A has made sure those pigs are in blankets this year."

Wortel forced a smile onto his face which Chief Superintendent Archibald took as him being mightily impressed with Mrs A's efforts.

"Boss," called out Dorothy, who now had the same look on her face as Oranges and Lemons.

'Oh crikey,' thought Wortel. 'Please don't say she is

catching their stupid gene'.

"What's wrong Dorothy?"

"You need to see this. The boys were processing the driving license we found at the crime scene and we've hit an access denied message. We don't have sufficient security."

"What?!" exclaimed Wortel.

"Ah, I can help out with that actually," interjected Archibald. "In fact, that's what I am doing back in the office. You tried to process that before the session with the prunes didn't you?"

Oranges and Lemons nodded.

"Well, when I got back to my office I had an urgent call from the Food Sapiens Secret Service, MI GasMark5. It seems that our dead body is a secret agent and a Mince Spy to boot. The head of MI GasMark5 is coming across personally to meet us. He sounded rather peeved and he wants the body back."

"Now steady on," said Wortel. "This is our crime scene."

Archibald held up a hand which caused Wortel to stop mid-rant.

"Wortel, Wortel, Wortel. MI GasMark5 outranks us.

We haven't a chance of stopping them taking over if that is what they want to do."

"So we just give up then?" said Dorothy despondently.

"I never said that at all," replied Archibald, a devilish smile developing on his face.

Dorothy and Wortel looked at each other. They had never seen Archibald like this before.

"Sir, you've lost us," muttered Wortel.

"We haven't given up team. Not at all. Now we play dirty."

****

The head of MI GasMark5 bounded through reception flashing his identification quickly to the surprised staff who manned the desk. Ignoring the lifts, he and his entourage found the stairs and began taking them two at a time. Reaching the floor he needed, he burst through the doors and headed for the Food Related Crime offices.

"Ho, Ho, Ho, my name is Nicholas Claus and I am the head of MI GasMark5, the Food Sapiens Secret Service," he boomed as strode purposefully into the Food Related Crime offices. "I understand you have one of my agents. I want him back and I want all of the evidence you have collected. I have with me disclaimers which you will all sign and you will never speak of this case again. Do I make myself clear?"

Chief Superintendent Archibald stood waiting to greet this most unwelcome of visitors.

"My name is Chief Superintendent Archibald and I am the accountable officer for this crime unit. Firstly, I understand protocol and when that has been followed all of my officers will be happy to sign the disclaimers. However, you have not yet identified your alleged agent and therefore we cannot confirm whether he or she is dead or alive."

Nicholas Claus was not used to being spoken to in his manner and he began stroking his long, fluffy white beard which his staff knew to be a sign of unhappiness. Turning away from Chief Superintendent Archibald he considered his options.

"I can make things very uncomfortable for this unit and all those who work within it," he said not looking directly at Archibald.

"Right back at ya."

Nicholas Claus spun on the spot shaking his belly like a bowl full of jelly.

"Do you know who you are talking to?"

"I do. This is why I am prepared to send a press release to the Daily Melancholy giving them an update on the road traffic accident which occurred last night. I think the readers of the Daily Melancholy will be most perturbed by this breaking news."

The rosy cheeks which adorned Nicholas Claus' face started to fade. "What road traffic accident?"

"A young maiden by the name of Snow White was waiting for some friends, innocently passing the time of night without a care in the world when a motorised sleigh, driven by an out of control drunk reindeer mounted the pavement, hitting her and another vehicle."

Nicholas Claus lunged for his back pocket, pulling his wallet from his large red trousers. He thumbed through his store cards and realised the one for Widdle was missing.

"I'll bloody kill him," he roared before storming out of the office.

9

The not so secret Santa

Nicholas Claus had returned to the Food Related Crime office looking calmer than he had a few minutes earlier. In his hand he carried a long thin case which he rested on the edge of Wortel's desk. Slipping off his large red coat, he drooped that over the back of Wortel's chair before giving a signal to his entourage. As one they upped and left the office, closing the door behind them leaving Nicholas Claus and the Food Related Crime team alone.

"I think we got off on the wrong foot, no offence intended," Nicholas Claus said pointing towards Archibald's false leg.

"None taken."

"Good. This whole thing has come as a massive shock to us all. The death of an agent weighs heavy on the shoulders especially when you were the one that sent him into action."

Nicholas Claus paused for a few moments looking off into space as he gathered his thoughts. Oranges and Lemons thought he had spotted something on the ceiling and started looking for it as well until Dorothy clumped them both around the back of the head.

"The agent who was murdered at Goodeatery is called Mitchell. He is, no, sorry, was, an excellent Mince Spy and would go undercover for eleven months of the year only resurfacing around December. I trusted him like no other agent and his death pains me. I want his murderer caught and caught quickly. That is why I want the case handed over to the Food Sapiens Secret Service. But, and I understand your position Chief Superintendent Archibald, my old friend Rudolph has thrown a spanner in the works."

Nicholas Claus walked away from Wortel's desk and began pacing the room.

"What I am about to do is unprecedented. I want the charges against Rudolph to be dropped. I will take care of him after all of the Christmas presents are delivered. He is my problem and I will make sure it is resolved. In return, I will share this case with you. Full disclosure from your team. Full disclosure from my team. Is that a deal Chief Superintendent?"

Nicholas Claus extended his hand towards Archibald, who himself stepped forward.

"How can we be sure we will get full disclosure from your team?" Archibald pressed, playing hardball with the man they now knew to be the infamous Secret Santa.

"Because Claudette is already on her way here to be interviewed by your team. Make no mistake Archibald, I know you have a talented team and I respect what you have achieved."

Archibald ignored the flattery. "Claudette?"

"Yes. She is another of my agents. She is a clandestine cranberry and also Mitchell's lover. I have told her to answer all of your questions frankly wherever that may lead."

Archibald considered what he heard, extended his hand, and made the deal with Secret Santa.

"Now, one last thing," Nicholas said as he picked up his coat. "Can I see Rudolph please?"

As the team filed out of the Food Related Crime office towards the lift in order to take Nicholas Claus to where Rudolph was being held, nobody noticed that sitting on the edge of Wortel's desk was the long, thin case that Nicholas Claus had placed there just a few minutes earlier.

****

As they waited for the lift, Lemons tugged at Nicholas Claus big red coat.

"Excuse me Santa, can I ask you something?"

"Of course little fellow. Ask anything you like. Would you like to sit on my knee? Ho, Ho, Ho."

Lemons eyed Santa suspiciously. "I'll take a rain check on that thanks," he said not hiding the nervousness that had appeared in his voice. "No, I wanted to ask whether you can fly anywhere in the world you want?"

"Yes I can."

"And you can get anything you want, any time?"

Nicholas Claus was becoming a little impatient with Lemons and also the lift which was taking forever to arrive.

"Yes. What's your point?"

"Why do you have a Widdle store card? I mean, why Widdle? Are you someone who is incontinent?"

Everyone looked at Nicholas Claus while taking a step back and checking the floor.

"Ho, Ho, Ho," he cried. "No, I am on an undercover mission myself. I have discovered that some of my staff are moonlighting at Widdle and I have been trying to catch them out."

Everyone breathed a sigh of relief. No wet feet today.

"Any luck with that?" asked Lemons.

"Yes actually. I've found some of my toymakers were working at Widdle and were becoming overzealous in giving out orders."

"Doing what?" asked Dorothy, intrigued with where this was heading.

"You'll never guess," he said as the lift finally arrived and the doors opened.

"No I won't," she replied. "What were they doing?"

Nicholas Clause laughed once more as he stepped into the lift with Chief Superintendent Archibald and Detective Inspector Wortel. As the doors began to close he looked at Dorothy and winked.

"Elf and safety."

****

Rudolph was sobering up pretty quickly. As he stood in his cell and looked at portly figure that stared back at him he decided that he could still pass off for being drunk for one last song.

"Oh Jingle Bells, Santa smells

Working at Widdle all day
Ankle deep in piss
Life ain't no bliss
But what can people say, hey…"

10

A clandestine cranberry

With a semi-sober Rudolph escorted from the premises by Nicholas Claus, the head honcho of the Food Sapiens Secret Service and the man now known to be Secret Santa, Wortel and Dorothy sat in a small interview room opposite a young, bright red little cranberry who answered to the name of Claudette.

It was clear Claudette had been crying as juice marks ran all down her shiny peel. Dorothy handed her a tissue and rested her hand on Claudette's giving it a small squeeze. Not too hard mind as they didn't want cranberry sauce marks in the interview room, which had just been redecorated a fetching shade of shocking pink. Thinking that it would be rude to interview Claudette in sunglasses, Wortel removed them from his face, squinted at the brightness of the walls and tentatively began his interview.

"I understand Nicholas Claus has explained why you are here?"

Claudette nodded, seemingly too upset to speak at this stage.

"We are truly sorry for your loss. I want to assure you that we will do everything we can to bring whoever did this to justice."

Another nod.

"You've worked for the Food Sapiens Secret Service for how long now?"

"Four years."

"And you've known Mitchell all of that time?"

"No. Just for the last eighteen months."

"What can you tell us about the work of the Secret Service?"

"Well, we normally wouldn't discuss specifics but Mr Claus has said on this occasion I can make an exception. What would you like to know?"

"What active cases you are working on. What cases Mitchell was working on. Anything you think might be relevant."

Claudette took a moment as she thought how best to respond without breaching any national secrets. Wortel studied her face and saw the grief lines etched around her eyes and mouth. He also noticed she had composed herself slightly and that she would be able to give them the information they sought.

"I have been working on two cases recently. One has just ended but the other is ongoing. I had been working with other food sapiens on the apparent disappearance of Hector, some beluga caviar, who we think has defected to Russia. I went undercover with food sapiens agents from the custard division, the sponge finger division and the cream division, but things never worked out how we expected."

"How come?"

"One thing went wrong after another and we ended up in a trifle difficulty."

Wortel and Dorothy exchanged looks as Claudette continued.

"My on-going case is working with Morag, a fine strong Dundee cake. She is undercover trying to infiltrate groups who want to create an independent food sapiens state within the UK. She is doing a fine job right now but I can't see how that is connected to the murder of Mitchell."

Wortel hated to admit it, but neither could he.

"And what about any cases Mitchell was working on?"

"Ah yes, now this is where I think we may have a lead," she said, becoming more animated than she had at any time during the interview. "Mitchell was investigating Earl Grey, the tea baron."

"The Earl Grey!" exclaimed Dorothy.

"The very one."

Dorothy suddenly looked slightly flushed.

"What's up with you?" asked Wortel.

"Nothing, nothing," she replied rather too quickly. "Just that I was reading a book of his recently."

"Fifty Shades of Earl Grey?" asked Claudette.

Dorothy blushed.

"Don't worry. It's doing the rounds at the Secret Service now. What number are you up?"

"Forty-two."

Wortel hadn't heard of this book at all and while the

ladies were talking he had quickly scanned the internet for information. He found the page he was seeking.

"Says here it is an erotic book," he said.

"Not your sort of thing," Dorothy replied.

"Come on, I'm no prude. What's number forty-two when it's at home?"

"The shade of Earl Grey number forty-two is Gnat's Piss."

"And what's so erotic about that?" said Wortel looking increasingly confused.

Dorothy and Claudette exchanged a look before Wortel's human colleague answered.

"Number forty-two, Gnat's Piss. What looks uninspiring and weak on the outside might be different when you get it in your mouth."

As Wortel blushed yellow, the colour carrots turn when embarrassed, there was a knock at the door and Dr Richards entered.

"Wortel, I've found something. May I have a word please?

Wortel quickly waved Dr Richards into the interview room and encouraged her to sit down.

"Dr Richards, this is Claudette who works at the Food Sapiens Secret Service. She is helping us with our enquiries into Mitchell's death. We've agreed with Nicholas Claus that there will be full disclosure, so anything you've found we can share."

Wortel turned to Claudette. "Would you mind reporting this information to Nicholas Claus?"

"Of course," she said, taking out a small notepad and pen.

Dr Richards nodded and opened her folder.

"I was conducted my preliminary autopsy report when I found a strange mark on the back of Mitchell's neck. It seemed to be a small scratch to his shortcrust skin and on further examination I found it was a needle mark."

Wortel held up his hand to stop Dr Richards.

"How on earth did you see that? I mean he was quite badly burnt."

Claudette let out a gasp, her hand trembling at what Wortel had said. Feeling his stomach knot at his own insensitivity, Wortel mumbled an apology before turning back to Dr Richards.

"The griddle to which Mitchell was tied meant that not all of his shortcrust pastry was as damaged as the rest of him. We caught a break in that the needle mark was on a part of his neck that ended up protected to some degree by the griddle. Anyway, that's not all."

Dr Richards broke out into a large smile, which she often had to do in order to fill her overly large face. Against the backdrop of the shocking pink wall she was quite the sight.

"When I found the needle mark I immediately stopped the autopsy and tried to find out if he was drugged. So I took a sample of his mincemeat to toxicology and asked them to fast track the results. And he was drugged. Serotonin."

"And what's that?" asked Wortel.

"No idea. I've never heard of it before. Toxicology is going to try and get to the bottom of it but they are pretty snowed under at the moment."

Claudette sat forward. "I've heard of Serotonin but I can't remember why. Wortel, can I head back to my department please and I will call you as soon as I have some news?"

"Yes, good idea."

After Claudette and Dr Richards had left the interview room Wortel and Dorothy sat looking at each other.

"Dorothy," he said quietly. "I haven't a clue what's going on here."

"I know the feeling," she replied. "What do you think we should do next?"

"Tea," he replied.

"Good idea. I'll have an extra scoop of sugar in mine."

"No, don't be daft. I mean tea. Earl Grey. I think we should pay him a visit."

Dorothy sat upright in her seat and started running her hand through her hair getting it into place.

"Now you're talking Wortel. Now you're talking."

****

Wortel and Dorothy walked back into the Food Related Crime offices to find them completely empty. Oranges and Lemons were nowhere to be seen.

"Have they left for good do you think?" Wortel asked hopefully as he sat himself back down at his desk.

Dorothy had herself walked across to the team whiteboard and had removed a note which they had left for her.

"No such luck," she replied. "They've left a note to say that they were reviewing the CCTV and have stopped it an interesting point which they think we should look at. They said they will be back later but they got a call from the head of auditioning at Jack and the Baked Bean Stalker. He wanted to see them so they have rushed off."

Wortel sat back in his seat and shook his head. In the middle of a murder investigation his two fruit officers had rushed off to a pantomime audition. Shocking. And yet more shocking was that for some reason it didn't surprise him as much it probably should have done.

Who Killed The Mince Spy?

11

Earl Grey has gone away

"Shall we check the CCTV now or when we come back from Earl Grey's?" Dorothy asked.

"The last time they wanted us to look at something interesting they found on CCTV, it turned out to be a dog and his owner who looked alike. They found that funny for days," replied Wortel, the tone of his voice already answering Dorothy's question.

Dorothy pulled a pained expression remembering the incident only too well.

"Later it is then," she said as she picked up her handbag and headed for the exit.

Wortel stood from his desk and was about to follow his colleague when he saw the small, thin box that had been left on the edge of his desk. Adorning the case, in gold lettering, were the initials N.C.

"What's that?" Dorothy queried heading over to Wortel who was looking all around the casing.

"Not a foggiest, but it seems it belongs to Nicholas Claus."

"Are you going to open it?"

"Dorothy Knox! Do you think I am going to open the personal belongings of the head of the Food Sapiens Secret Service?"

Dorothy's jaw set and she fixed Wortel with a glowering look.

"Okay," he replied. "Of course I am going to open it."

Unhooking the lock, Wortel lifted the lid and saw inside a long, sharp syringe and a small bottle which contained what appeared to be a white, yellowy substance.

****

The short drive to Earl Grey's home was conducted in silence. Dorothy drove while Wortel stared out of the window thinking about the syringe that remained on the edge of his desk.

Was Nicholas Claus somehow involved in this affair?

****

As they approached the large town house belonging to Earl Grey, Wortel and Dorothy noticed the street had been blocked off by a string of police cars. Just beyond the cordon were a number of large police vans, normally reserved for incidents involving large crowds.

Dorothy parked the car and walked with Wortel towards the scene. Wortel took out his identification and flashed it at the officer who was preventing passers-by from walking through.

"You get a kick out of that don't you?"

"Might," said Wortel a definite spring in his step.

"Power corrupts you know."

As the food sapiens detective and his homo sapiens sergeant arrived outside of Earl Grey's home the police were carting off twelve drummers drumming, eleven pipers piping, ten lords a-leaping and nine ladies dancing. Of those, Wortel noticed that they were carrying seven swans a-swimming, albeit without water so it was quite difficult, six geese a-laying, some of the ladies – five in fact – had gold rings. Wortel also thought he saw four calling birds, three French hens and two turtle doves.

He turned to Dorothy. "Thank God there wasn't a

partridge in a pear tree," he said. "That would've conjured up memories of 'Addicted to Death' – our last story which was published."

"Wouldn't it just," said Dorothy. "And to think, that's another reference to our debut book that's been made in this short story. Do you think we could get in any more references?"

"I think that's pushing it," replied Wortel. "Don't want to upset the readers too much."

"Fair point," she acknowledged. "Back to this story."

Wortel called across to the lead police officer. "Have you got everybody out?"

"Everyone that we could find," he replied. "There was one group that got away. Around eight females. If you see them do let us know as soon as possible."

"What's wrong with them?" Wortel asked signalling to the drummers drumming, the pipers piping, the lords a-leaping, the ladies dancing who were carrying swans a-swimming, geese a-laying, while wearing gold rings, as well as holding calling birds, French hens and turtle doves. But for the record, not a partridge in a pear tree.

"To be frank, they are smacked off their faces. Drugs of some kind, not sure what though. We've never seen behaviour like this. The neighbour called it in." The police office nodded to the building next door where the curtain flicked closed as Dorothy looked in that direction.

"He said he was fed up with the noise since Earl Grey rushed off abroad."

"Abroad?" asked Wortel.

"Yes. He is a frequent visitor to China apparently and he rushed off early hours this morning. The neighbour said there was a little bit of disturbance last night. Seems someone was trying to get into the flats to speak to Earl Grey but he wouldn't answer. Then first thing this morning, Earl Grey has rushed off to China. We've checked immigration and they have confirmed his departure on a private jet."

"Did the neighbour get a description by any chance?"

"Not a good one. Said he saw a lot of white, but couldn't see too much more. He said he thought he heard a soft rustling noise though, he thought maybe even castanets."

"Castanets? Really?"

The police officer looked at Wortel. "Yes that's what he said but I wouldn't rely on it too much. I mean after all, how could you distinguish castanets over the sound of the twelve drummers drumming, eleven pipers piping, ten lords a-leaping and nine ladies dancing. And of those…"

"Yes, yes," said Wortel turning on his heel quickly. "I think we know how that one ends."

12

Flash bang wallop, oh what a picture

"Are you thinking what I am thinking?" Dorothy asked as she pulled the car away from Earl Grey's home.

"That you want to put the Engleburger Humperdinck CD on the radio again?"

"No," she replied, although she never admitted that the thought had crossed her mind. "I was thinking about what the neighbour saw. Lots of white at Earl Grey's door. Could be a long beard you know. And we found the syringe in the office. Wortel. It's all pointing towards Nicholas Claus, you know that don't you?"

Wortel did know that. And he had no good response so left the question hanging in the air like a bad smell. The kind you get when cauliflower has been stewed. Or just cooked actually.

****

Arriving back at the office they found Oranges and Lemons still absent. Neither Wortel nor Dorothy was complaining.

"Look. I'm going to call Nicholas Claus," Wortel said. "You check the CCTV."

Wortel closed the main door to the office so they would not be disturbed and settled himself at his desk for what was not going to be an easy conversation. Dorothy found the CCTV footage on her emails, slipped off her shoes, swung her legs up onto her desk and clicked play.

"Ho, Ho, Hullo," boomed the jolly voice of Nicholas Claus.

"Sir, hello, its Detective Inspector Wortel here."

"Wortel, good timing. I have just been briefed by Claudette and I have some news I need to share with you urgently."

"That's good," replied Wortel, steadying himself for what he was about to say. "Can I just ask a couple of questions first please?"

"Of course, go ahead."

"Where were you last night?"

Wortel sensed the change in the tone of Nicholas Claus voice. "I was at home with Mrs Claus trying to sober up Rudolph. What on earth makes you ask?"

Ignoring the question Wortel continued. "And sir, what's the purpose of the syringe you carry about with you. You know, the one in the case which you left at my office in error."

"Ah, now I can see what you are getting at Wortel. You wonder if I have anything to do with this affair. You are right, I did leave the case in error, but please do have it checked out. You'll see that it is insulin. I am a diabetic Wortel, which shouldn't come as that much of a surprise. Look at the size of me and think about what I have to eat when I do my yearly rounds. Cakes everywhere. Does anybody ever leave me a nice piece of fruit or a salad? No, it's cakes, cakes and more cakes. Ho, Ho, Ho."

As Wortel considered what he was hearing, Dorothy had come across the section of the CCTV which Oranges and Lemons had found interesting. Jumping up from her desk, she waved at Wortel to get his attention.

"Boss, get me on speakerphone quickly."

"Er, Mr Claus, sorry to do this but I need to put

you on speakerphone. My sergeant Dorothy Knox has something she needs to share."

"Go ahead."

Wortel pressed the telephone button and signalled to Dorothy to speak.

"Hello Mr Claus. We have some interesting CCTV footage. You'll know that the speed cameras have been reduced to 15mph what with the mobility scooter drag racing."

"Ah yes," said Nicholas Claus. "Makes getting to Widdle for my undercover work quite the challenge."

"Quite. Well, we have CCTV footage from outside of Goodeatery on the day of the murder. There are three people who have set off the speed cameras because they were running at over 20 mph."

Wortel's eyes widened. "Who can run that fast?"

It was Nicholas Claus that answered.

"Turkeys. It was Tarquinius Gallopava wasn't it Dorothy?"

Dorothy looked at Wortel with a stunned look on her face. How did he know?

"Yes. The flash of the camera lit them up wonderfully. Well, it lit him up, the other two it was difficult to say. One has a sombrero and, Wortel, get this; the other had his castanets above his head."

"I bet that hurt," said Wortel, pulling a face at Dorothy who did her best not to burst out laughing.

Nicholas Claus continued oblivious to the innuendo happening at the other end of the phone. "I know who they are. They are his turkey henchmen. They do the dirty work. And Wortel, the drug that Dr Richards found, serotonin. That is a natural mind-altering substance found in turkeys that causes contentment and sleepiness. We've suspected Tarquinius was up to something as we knew he and Earl Grey had links, but we never knew what the connection was. I sent Mitchell to investigate Earl Grey and it seems he stumbled onto something much bigger. When Dr Richards identified serotonin it fell into place. Tarquinius must be selling serotonin to Earl Grey who has spiced it up and given it to his friends. That will explain why we have drummers drumming, lords a-leaping…"

"Got that bit sir," said Wortel quickly before the whole thing started once more.

"Jolly good. I will hazard a guess that Earl Grey has not paid on his debts which is why he did a moonlight flit."

"That makes sense," Wortel agreed. "We'll get a call out for his arrest immediately."

"Not enough evidence Wortel," said Nicholas Claus. "We need more proof. Look, I've some calls I need to make. Keep me informed."

Dorothy looked at Wortel a concerned look on her face. "Boss, I think there is something else at play here."

"What's that Dorothy?"

"The referendum. I think he must have drugged the Minister for DAFaRT into agreeing to it. Do you remember he said on NewsFoodNight that he had a bruised arm."

"My God, Dorothy you're right. This whole affair is a sham. And to think, the population of this great country will be eating nut cutlets if we don't act fast."

"What do we do next?" she asked.

Wortel smiled at Dorothy. "I just so happen to be cooking up a plan."

13

Why do you build me up, buttercup?

"Do you think this was a good idea boss?"

Wortel smiled at Dorothy. "What makes you think that I haven't thought this through?"

They stood outside of Goodeatery waiting for Tarquinius Gallopava to arrive. Wortel had called the Pluck-It office and managed to speak with the Chief Turkey Gobbler in person. What Wortel had said led to Tarquinius gobbling away like a mad thing. This was either going to be a dream or an utter disaster.

"Did you manage to get hold of Oranges or Lemons?"

"No boss," Dorothy replied looking at the mobile phone which she held in her left hand. "I've called and left voice messages for them both but neither one has replied."

"Well that's them done for. I want them gone now."

Dorothy was on the verge of answering when a black limousine drove up, stopped and from the driver's seat out stepped Tarquinius Gallopava. He strutted around in a circle, locked the car and head bobbing backwards and forwards headed towards the two officers from the Food Crime team.

"Your call was most unpleasant DI Wortel. And frankly, an outright lie."

Wortel noticed how Tarquinius had kept his distance and was looking all around surveying the scene. Wortel had also noticed that he was alone and his two turkey henchmen were nowhere to be seen. He hoped the backup that Chief Superintendent Archibald had arranged had already picked them up.

"Chief Gobbler Gallopava, we have just a few questions to ask you about the murder of Mitchell the Mince Spy. We have evidence, which we stored behind us in Goodeatery which ties you to the scene."

"What evidence?"

"Why don't we go inside? Would you like to go first?"

"Unless you tell me what evidence you have, this

meeting is over DI Wortel."

Wortel set out his lie once more.

"We found feathers. Long white downy feathers all over the oven in which Mitchell was overbaked. We are confident that we can match those feathers to your coat."

"Liar!" screamed Tarquinius, his temper flaring. "I never put that Mince Spy into the oven. That was done by men."

"Thank you for the confession," smiled Wortel. "Did you get that Dorothy?"

Dorothy held up the mobile phone in her hand which had recorded the conversation from the moment Tarquinius had arrived at Goodeatery. "Every word."

Wortel looked at the great figure of Tarquinius Gallopava who had started to expand his wings to their full capacity.

"And yes sir, for the record you are correct. We do not have feathers in Goodeatery, but we have your confession which will be much firmer evidence than the CCTV of you running away from the crime scene on the day of the murder."

Dorothy looked at Tarquinius who despite having

just made a confession to the two police officers seemed to suddenly relax. In fact, it wasn't just a smile that was developing on his face, but it was becoming full blown laughter. She looked at Wortel who also seemed to be distracted by the strange turn of events. And then, sounding distant to begin with, but getting ever nearer, was the distinct sound of someone shaking their castanets.

Wortel was the first to spin around finding himself face to face with a sombrero wearing turkey brandishing a syringe. Alongside him stood another turkey, not quite as tall, but shaking his castanets as though his life depended on it. Dorothy had also turned around and realising the danger they were in quickly typed a short text message.

Tarquinius Gallopava moved close and placed a soft, feathery arm on the shoulders of Wortel and Dorothy.

"Can I take it that the back up is no more?"

The turkey henchmen nodded.

"Excellent. Shall we dine?" he asked and directed the two Food Related Crime officers towards Goodeatery.

****

Lemons nudged Oranges sharply in the rear. "We've got a text from Dorothy. It says: 'IN TROUBLE. GOODEATERY. URGENT'.

"Right, we best go, besides this audition has gone on forever," said Oranges, who trotted off stage quickly with Lemons right behind him.

"Should we change first?" Lemons queried.

"Dorothy said urgent. I don't think there's time."

****

The turkey henchmen prised open the door to Goodeatery and pushed Wortel and Dorothy inside.

"This way," smiled Tarquinius. "I know just where I want you."

****

Oranges ran from the theatre audition and stopped sharply on the pavement. Lemons, who was just behind, ran straight into the back of him.

"Watch where you are going," cried Oranges.

"How can I?" Lemons wailed. "I can't see a thing in this outfit."

****

Tarquinius Gallopava stood in front on a large door sealed shut with a long bolt handle.

Detective Inspector Willie Wortel, for the first time in his life, said a silent goodbye to his loved ones.

****

A group of eight female fugitives sat huddled in the corner of a small cafe, when passing by right in front of them, ran a cow called Buttercup heading in the direction of Scottie Rodgers restaurant Goodeatery.

They paid their bill and headed out onto the street.

****

The door was unbolted and DI Wortel forced inside.

"And you can stand here and watch your boss freeze to death," whispered Tarquinius into the ear of Dorothy Knox, who stood, turkey henchmen on either side of her, powerless to help.

****

"Will you get your hands off my udders?" cried a somewhat pained Lemons.

"Eight maids a-milking," sang the eight maids a-milking.

****

The cold from the freezer room pierced Wortel's peel almost immediately.

He looked around to see if he could find anything to help keep him warm.

Nothing.

****

The chase was on.

The cow with the painful udders, played so admirably by Oranges and Lemons, had freed itself from the eight maids a-milking, and was sprinting towards Goodeatery.

The maids a-milking still felt they had some work to do and were in hot pursuit.

****

Brussels sprouts on a stick. Peas in pods. Mini sausage rolls.

All useless.

Wortel opened another crate and jumped back in horror.

Frozen carrots.

****

Dorothy began looking around hoping to find a way of helping Wortel.

Tarquinius pressed the syringe to her neck so she felt its point.

"Your time will come my dear."

'Where the hell are Oranges and Lemons?' she wondered to herself.

****

"Lemons, I can see Goodeatery. We're almost there."

"What about the maids a-milking?"

Oranges glanced over his shoulder. The eight maids who wanted to milk were making up ground.

"Keep running Lemons, I'll see if I can find an opening."

"You ought to be where I am," said Lemons, the back-end of the cow.

****

Wortel looked through the small window and saw the face of Dorothy Knox staring back at him.

She was crying.

"Goodbye," Wortel said, and sat down on the floor, the coldness having chilled him so much that he just wanted to sleep.

****

Oranges spotted the door which the turkey henchmen had forced open and he veered towards it.

Lemons felt his partner change direction and did his best to keep up, although it had slowed him down without a doubt.

As they entered Goodeatery, the maids a-milking pounced.

****

Dorothy Knox watched her boss, her friend, her confidant, Detective Inspector Willie Wortel mouth goodbye and sit down out of view. Her tears became sobs drowning out the sound of the castanets being played by the turkey henchmen to her right.

But her sobs did not drown out the commotion from further down the kitchen.

****

"For the last time Madam, get your hands off my udders. I am a fruit police officer, not a cow."

"Oh isn't she amusing," said one of the maids a-milking, yanking at the pantomime cow for all she was worth. "You are a lovely cow."

"Bullocks," replied Lemons.

"No a cow, really," the maid a-milking retorted.

****

Tarquinius Gallopava had to admit it. Never in all of his years had he stood in a restaurant kitchen with two other turkeys, one playing the castanets, one wearing a sombrero while a carrot detective was freezing to death in the store. And certainly never with a pantomime cow, being milked by eight maids, running straight for him.

****

The collision was epic.

Not only did feathers fly, but the head of the cow flew off Oranges and went straight up in the air. Lemons pulled himself out from his part of the costume and stood, half Lemon, half cow.

The maids a-milking, fearing the drugs given to them by Earl Grey had gone dangerously wrong, screamed and ran from Goodeatery as fast as their legs would carry them.

With the turkeys scrambling to their feet, Dorothy sensed her opportunity, ran forwards and grabbed the bolt which sealed the freezing cold store room. She pulled the door open and saw Wortel lying on the floor in a state of unconsciousness. She could only hope any warmth from the kitchen would be enough to bring him around.

****

Tarquinius was first to his feet and he swung his winged arms towards Oranges who managed to duck out of the way. Tarquinius gobbled, and stalked after the food sapiens officer. Lemons, watching his fellow fruit officer did what any half-dressed lemon-cum-cow would do and mooed.

It was enough to make Tarquinius stop and turn around giving Oranges the chance to escape.

****

The turkey henchman with the castanets was next to his

feet. Well for as long as it took for Dorothy to land a firm right hook to his jaw, sending him sprawling to floor.

God those castanets had annoyed her since they were first mentioned in Chapter One.

****

The turkey henchman with the sombrero did not last too much longer after that, for Oranges and Lemons grabbed a large roasting pan and together swung it with all of their might onto the top of his head as he was trying to gather his whereabouts.

He slumped back to the floor.

****

Tarquinius on the other hand was a much different proposition. He was taller, faster, and much more dangerous than the other two. And although Dorothy, Oranges and Lemons outnumbered him, they were in some danger.

Tarquinius battered away the roasting tin which Oranges and Lemons wielded and edged the three Food Related Crime officers towards a dark corner of the Goodeatery kitchen.

****

A strange sensation was coming over him.

There was feeling in his hands.

And his legs.

He was alive.

****

Dorothy pushed Oranges and Lemons behind her.

"The protective mother until the last," Tarquinius mocked. "But you are no match for me, the last bastion of freedom for the Turkey population."

****

'This will have to do' he thought to himself as he stepped back into the world.

'Now or never.'

****

Tarquinius had raised himself to his full height. With just a few blows from his wings and Dorothy, Oranges and Lemons would be no more.

"Can we just have one final comment?" Dorothy asked

of Tarquinius.

"Go ahead."

Dorothy looked at Oranges and Lemons and nodded. Although no words had been spoken between them, they all knew what to do.

"He's behind you!" they cried.

"Oh no he's not," he cried back dismissively.

"Oh yes I am," said a thawing Detective Inspector Wortel.

****

Tarquinius Gallopava spun on the spot and saw Wortel standing positioned, Brussels sprouts on a stick in hand, ready for action. Wielding it like a kendo stick, battle ensued.

****

Tarquinius began using his wings like chopping machines while Wortel matched his every move with the Brussels sprouts on a stick. And yet while Wortel was matching Tarquinius blow for blow, he seemed to be deliberately walking back from where he had just come.

****

Dorothy, Oranges and Lemons followed the battle as it moved back towards the freezer store room.

What on earth was Wortel up to?

And then she saw what he had left on the kitchen side for her.

****

As they approached the freezer room, Tarquinius noticed that his two turkey henchmen were missing.

He looked at Wortel, a flash of confusion crossing his face for the first time.

Wortel nodded towards the freezer room where on the floor lay the two unconscious turkey henchmen that Wortel had dragged in moments before.

An enraged Tarquinius roared and ran forwards, wings beating a path towards Wortel.

Wortel was expecting this reaction and threw the Brussels sprouts on a stick at Tarquinius.

As he fended that off, Wortel threw himself to the ground and onto the roasting tin which Oranges and Lemons had dropped in their earlier scuffle, sliding under Tarquinius who turned around 180 degrees to face Wortel.

And yet what he faced came as a surprise to which he was not expecting.

****

Dorothy, Oranges and Lemons were each armed with a round of podded peas attached to their hips.

Dorothy squeezed the tip of her podded pea and the shell broke open. Oranges and Lemons, having never fired podded vegetables before, watched her intently and followed her lead.

As Tarquinius went to charge she stepped forward and squeezed her pod hard, firing a small green bullet at the great turkey. It struck him firmly in the chest and he gobbled loudly. Now while the podded vegetables were never going to kill Tarquinius, they were certainly going to hurt him and force him backwards.

All three Food Related Crime officers began firing their podded vegetables at Tarquinius who took each round firmly in the chest and wings. Forced back with each shell, he eventually stumbled over something, losing his footing, falling to the ground.

And there beneath his feet, were his two turkey

henchmen.

"Cease fire," called Wortel as he raced to the freezer door, slamming it shut, before bringing the bolt firmly into place locking Tarquinius and his henchmen inside.

****

Outside of Goodeatery Wortel and his team slumped to the floor having narrowly escaped with their lives.

"You do realise there is a strong Christmas message to all this?" Wortel said.

"What's that?" they all asked him.

"Give peas a chance."

Who Killed The Mince Spy?

Epilogue

Summing up a Christmas cracker

Tarquinius Gallopava and his men were removed from the freezer by agents from MI GasMark5, when after defrosting, they were interrogated. Due to the Food Sapiens Intelligence Agency Bill the whereabouts of Tarquinius and his men cannot be disclosed although it is suspected that they ended up in Iceland.

****

Following the exposure of Tarquinius as an evil genius, the referendum result was quashed and the traditional turkey dinner was saved. Vegetarians, who believed this was the breakthrough moment their food regime needed, threw their arms up in despair and consoled themselves with a lettuce leaf.

****

Nicholas Claus, Rudolph and the other reindeers delivered all of the Christmas presents in a record time. Nicholas Claus did however suffer a hypoglycaemic attack on the delivery due to the number of mince pies, cakes and other sweet dishes he sampled.

****

Rudolph has been dry for the past thirty days.

****

Nicholas Claus was sufficiently impressed with the Food Related Crime team that he agreed to cut them into all relevant future cases. The cases were likely to occur when sufficient Christmas cracker jokes have been read and incorporated into a future adventure.

****

Sir Rupert Irksome has not yet returned from Coventry.

****

Snow White was released from hospital and is on the road to recovery. The same cannot be said for Scottie Rodgers who continues to receive daily physiotherapy although he hopes to be released in time for a cameo in any future Food

Related Crime short story.

****

The six dwarf cabbages involved in the road traffic accident recovered from their bruising, although the bad odour which follows them persists. Sleepy attended Widow Twanky's driving school where he was found to suffer from narcolepsy. Grumpy is attending anger management classes and Sneezy is receiving treatment for acute allergies. Happy is off his face on poppers.

****

With thanks to Mrs Archibald the pigs in blankets have been kept warm and there are no reported cases of pneumonia. The pigs in blankets were able to go undercover in the Arctic Circle where it has been discovered that chilli peppers are trying to melt the ice cap. They were allowed into the Arctic Circle as people thought that because of their name, they were from a cold food sapiens community.

****

Jack and the Baked Bean Stalker was a roaring success. Buttercup stole the show each night, mainly because it kept appearing on stage whenever it wanted to, even when not needed.

****

The prunes with the runes submitted their invoice but haven't yet been paid

****

Earl Grey has not yet returned to the UK as he is on a slow boat from China. When he does arrive he may show up in a Food Related Crime story called 'A chai for a chai'.

****

Wortel invited his team around on Christmas evening for an eggnog or two. Or in Dorothy's case, around seven or eight.

****

Dorothy remains the most normal member of the Food Related Crime team.

****

Depending on whichever one Redford can be bothered to write next, the Food Related Crime team will return in:

- • 'Nuts About Murder'
- • 'The Codfather'
- • 'The Cheese Olympics'

Or maybe none of the above and in something else completely different…

Also by Matthew Redford

www.matthewredford.com